to
Issy, Ed, Theo, Ruby, Grace, and Tom

Santa would like to thank elves Higgins, Hawkley, Smith, and Snow Jr. of the Color Department, who all worked on a selection of beaten-up, old computers. Santa was unable to upgrade them to new G5 workstations due to all the money he had to spend on the children.

ALADDIN PAPERBACKS
An imprint of Simon & Schuster Children's Publishing Division
1230 Avenue of the Americas, New York, NY 10020
Copyright © 2004 by Alan Snow
Also available in an Atheneum Books for Young Readers hardcover edition.
Designed by Polly Kanevsky
The text of this book was set in Lomba.
The illustrations for this book were rendered in pen and ink, with computer colorization.
Manufactured in China   1116 SCP
First Aladdin Paperbacks edition October 2007
6 8 10 9 7 5
The Library of Congress has cataloged the hardcover edition as follows:
Snow, Alan.
How Santa really works / by Alan Snow.—1st ed.
p. cm.
Summary: Santa Claus has a complicated and sophisticated Christmas operation, which includes the training of and numerous jobs for his elves to the celebrations at his own Christmas Day party.
ISBN-13: 978-0-689-85817-8 (hc)
ISBN-10: 0-689-85817-5 (hc)
[1. Santa Claus—Fiction. 2. Elves—Fiction. 3. Christmas—Fiction.] I. Title.
PZ7.S6805San 2004
[E]—dc22 2003019370
ISBN-13: 978-1-4169-5000-4 (pbk)
ISBN-10: 1-4169-5000-1 (pbk)

How Santa Really Works

By Alan Snow

ALADDIN PAPERBACKS · NEW YORK LONDON TORONTO SYDNEY

Have you ever wondered about Santa?

Where does he live?

How does he know what you want?

How does he get all the presents made and delivered?

And how does he know if you've been good?

There are a thousand questions you could ask about Santa. This book is here to explain all there is to know about Santa and his international operations. We'll start with . . .

Where does Santa live?

Santa (or Father Christmas, as he is also known) lives under the North Pole. He has a small, comfortable home beneath the snow and ice. Each morning after he wakes up he gets out of bed, has a bath, gets dressed, makes breakfast, and then goes downstairs to start work.

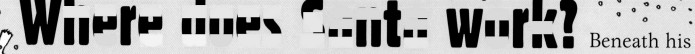

Where does Santa work?

Beneath his apartment is everything he needs to make Christmas happen. There are factories, warehouses, transport facilities, a communications center, and many other vital and necessary departments. This book covers all these departments, explaining what they do and how they work.

Who helps Santa?

Santa has many helpers. Most of these are elves. Elves live all over the world, but when they grow up, a lot of them get jobs with Santa and move to the North Pole. Each year more elves are recruited. The new elves must undergo extensive training before they start work. This is done at the C.C.E.,* the school where they learn all about Christmas. First the elves take a general class called Christmas 101. Then they choose one of the many different courses available at the college. These courses teach them how to do a specific job in one of the departments.

Welcome to the C.C.E.! I hope you enjoy your training. There are many careers that you can train for here.

Reindeer Medicine
Toy Sciences
Navigation
Flight Control
Computer Skills
Transport Logistics
Elf Resource Management
Tool Operation and Safety
Surveillance and Intelligence
Network Maintenance
Design and Technology
Complaint Handling
Wish Fulfillment
Weather Forecasting

I want to go into computers.

No! Toy Sciences sounds much more fun.

I want to look after reindeer.

They smell. I want a desk job.

I want to be a weatherman.

* Christmas College for Elves

How does Santa know what you want?

In the months leading up to Christmas, children write to Santa to tell him what they want. This is a very good idea because if he doesn't know what you want, he will have to guess. Santa is probably better than anybody else at guessing what children want, but it really is worth sending him a letter.

Dear Santa, I would like a chocolate cake, some muffins, a jar of blueberry jelly, eight bars of chocolate . . . I wondered if you could get me a real working submarine! I know this is the fifth time I have asked for the same thing, but I really, really like socks. A blue bike would be fantastic, but if it is not possible, I would like a baby hippo. Yours sincerely, Ed

Dear Santa, I would like an alligator, a truck full of cakes, and fifteen new pairs of sunglasses.

Love, John

Dear Santa, could you please send me a new brain so I could understand math? If not, could you send me a go-cart and some paintbrushes? Thank you! Zach

Dear Santa Claus, is it possible to send me a very dangerous chemistry set and a set of flameproof clothes? Very truly yours, Grace

Dear Father Christmas, please see the attached list. I cannot wait till Christmas, so please forward all the presents to me right now. I shall expect them tomorrow. Most sincerely, Isabel

Dear Santa, I have been very good. Can I have as many pairs of socks as you can manage? I hear that lots of peo don't like socks, so can I have theirs as well? I will be ver happy, as I have a huge collection and I am always on the lookout for new and more interesting socks.
Yours faithfully,
Brian

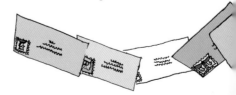

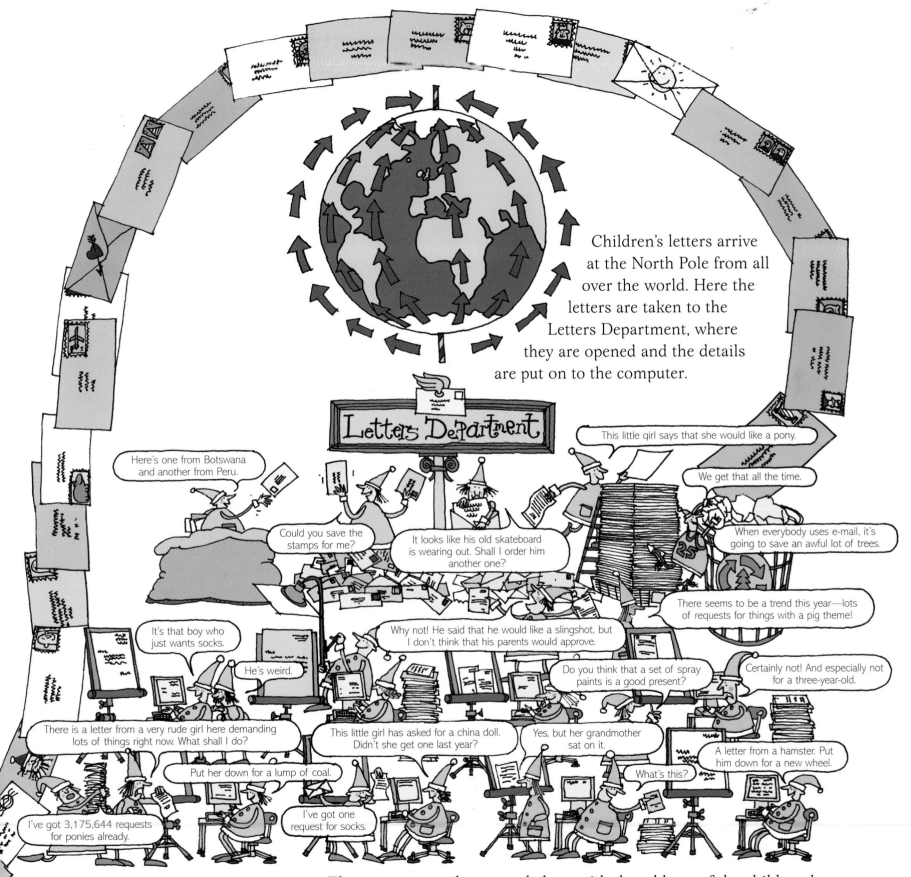

Children's letters arrive at the North Pole from all over the world. Here the letters are taken to the Letters Department, where they are opened and the details are put on to the computer.

The requests are then stored along with the address of the child, and this file is used to help organize toy production and delivery. This, of course, is dependent on children being good!

Christmas Intelligence Agency

How does Santa know if you have been good?

This is done for Santa by the CIA—the Christmas Intelligence Agency. All over the world, an elite squad of elves gathers data on children. It then relays the information to the CIA's offices back at the North Pole. Not only do the elves check on children to see if they are good, but they can also help Santa with information to help him guess what children might like, if they have not written to him.

Have you seen the list of what this boy did just on Thursday the fifth between 5:30 and 5:45?

What about the zoo animals?

They got them back in the end.

His poor parents!

This child, Henry Peabody, has improved since last year.

Would you believe it? This boy has been good that the computer can't register hi

What did he do last year?

What are you going to do, then?

You don't want to know, but it included a pot of glue and some sausages.

If she paints the cat like she says she will, there'll be no presents for her.

I'll get him into the system by markir that he eats too many bananas.

Shall I mark this one down for never brushing his teeth?

It's that kid who picks his nose all the time.

The CIA elves are trained in "Covert Surveillance"—this means hiding and spying on people. Elves enjoy this very much as they have a lot of fun with the camouflage.

When they have finished training, they are sent out all over the world to start work. As you will see on the next page, they are very busy.

Where do all the toys come from?

All the toys that come from Santa come from his Toy Department. This is divided into two main sections. The first department is Research and Development. This is where the toys are invented. A lot of toys come from ideas sent in by children. The rest are invented here. It can take quite a long time to go from the idea stage to a finished toy. Sometimes years!

> I think we could make it out of wood, and then if we painted it luminous blue, it would look cool and you could see it coming back at night.

> I think you should add wheels.

> How about feathers?

> If we made it from toffee, you could eat it when you finished playing with it.

> And if it was injection molded, we could eat all the bits that leaked out the side.

Brainstorming

The Research and Development Department is divided into four sections. The first is brainstorming. This is where elves sit down with Santa and think up the ideas. They also look at the ideas that children have sent in.

Design

The second section is Design. This is where more elves work out how to make the toys in a practical way. They have to understand materials, manufacturing, and children. They must also be able to draw.

Prototyping

The plans and instructions for the new toys are then sent to a section called Prototyping. This is where the first toy of a new design is made. The elf engineers have to be very skilled at all sorts of things. They must be able to sew, make models, do engineering, paint, make molds, be good with electronics, to name just a few. They are real craftsmen.

Testing

When a new toy (or "prototype," as it is called) is finished, it is sent to the Testing Section. Here it is tested for fun, safety, and reliability. If it passes all these tests, then it will be put into production (they will start making it in the factory). If it fails any of the tests, it is sent back to the Design Department for improvements. If it fails all of the tests, its parts will be recycled and the plans thrown away.

Where are all the toys made?

The second section of the Toy Department is probably the most important part of Santa's world. This is the Toy Factory, or Production Department, as it is called. It operates around the clock—twenty-four hours a day, seven days a week. Elves work an eight-hour shift everyday. It is a good place to work, as the elves know the joy the toys will bring. They chat and sing and sometimes one of the elves will read stories to everyone over the public address system.

What's a spongy wack bat?

We need another 36,000 teddy bears, please!

Can you send upstairs for some more heads?

You hold that until I am ready.

When the toys are finished, they are inspected and, if they pass, are then sent to the Storage Department.

Where are all the toys kept?

Deep beneath the ice there is a gigantic cave where all the toys are stored. It is a magical place where mountains of toys cover many, many square miles of floor. Every toy that has ever been delivered by Santa has, at one time or another, been stored there. At last count, that is over 976,592,331,684,078 toys.

Could you tell me where to put clockwork submarines?

Yes, they go over there with the small boats.

If you walk for about half an hour in that direction, you will see a golden hill in the distance. Those are teddy bears. It takes another half hour to get there.

Where shall I put these?

Non-fragile

Teams of elves who specialize in organization separate the toys into piles. When orders come in over the address system, these elves fetch the toys.

Before the toys leave the Storage Department, they are carefully wrapped up and labeled. Then they are sent to Dispatch.

Who organizes all the presents?

As Christmas approaches, it becomes time to get the toys ready to send out. This is done in Dispatch. Orders are printed out from the central computer, and the head dispatcher reads out the orders into a microphone connected to the Storage Department. Storage then sends the orders through.

And how do the elves know where to send the toys?

Each letter or file about a child has his or her address on it. The elves have a special invisible coding system. This gives the position of each house in the world. Using this code, the elves pack the parcels into batches for Santa to deliver. Each batch is packed into a numbered sack. The numbered sacks are then sent off to the Transport Department.

Boy | Girl

Transport

The rabbit goes around the tree. . . .

Could you make sure this year that you don't mix up Birmingham, Alabama, with Birmingham, England?!

It's an easy mistake to make!

No, it's not! They are thousands of miles apart!

Surely Santa can't get all the presents on his sleigh at once?

And how does he have enough time to keep flying to the North Pole and back? One of the best kept secrets about Santa is how he manages to get the presents delivered in time. The truth is, he has a lot of help. Elves load up lots of different crafts (or transporters) with as many presents as they can hold.

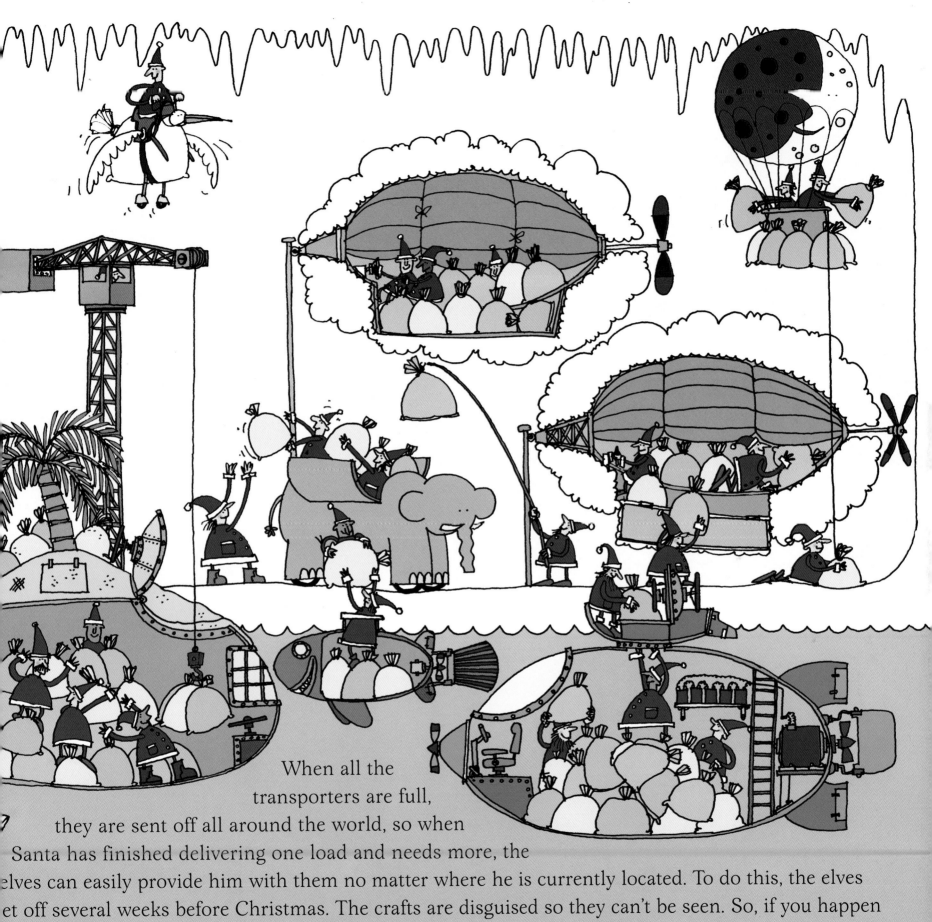

When all the transporters are full, they are sent off all around the world, so when Santa has finished delivering one load and needs more, the elves can easily provide him with them no matter where he is currently located. To do this, the elves set off several weeks before Christmas. The crafts are disguised so they can't be seen. So, if you happen to be sailing on a ship at Christmastime, keep an eye out for unexpected islands.

Santa's Sleighs

scale 1/60

Santa has, in fact, two sleighs: one for long distance work and the other for more crowded areas. These are built and maintained by the Transport Department elves.

Long Haul Sleigh (for open country)

helium bag

present sack

Santa

beard

windshield

elf

aileron

helium bag

helium bag

fuel tank

jet engine

runners

floatation deer

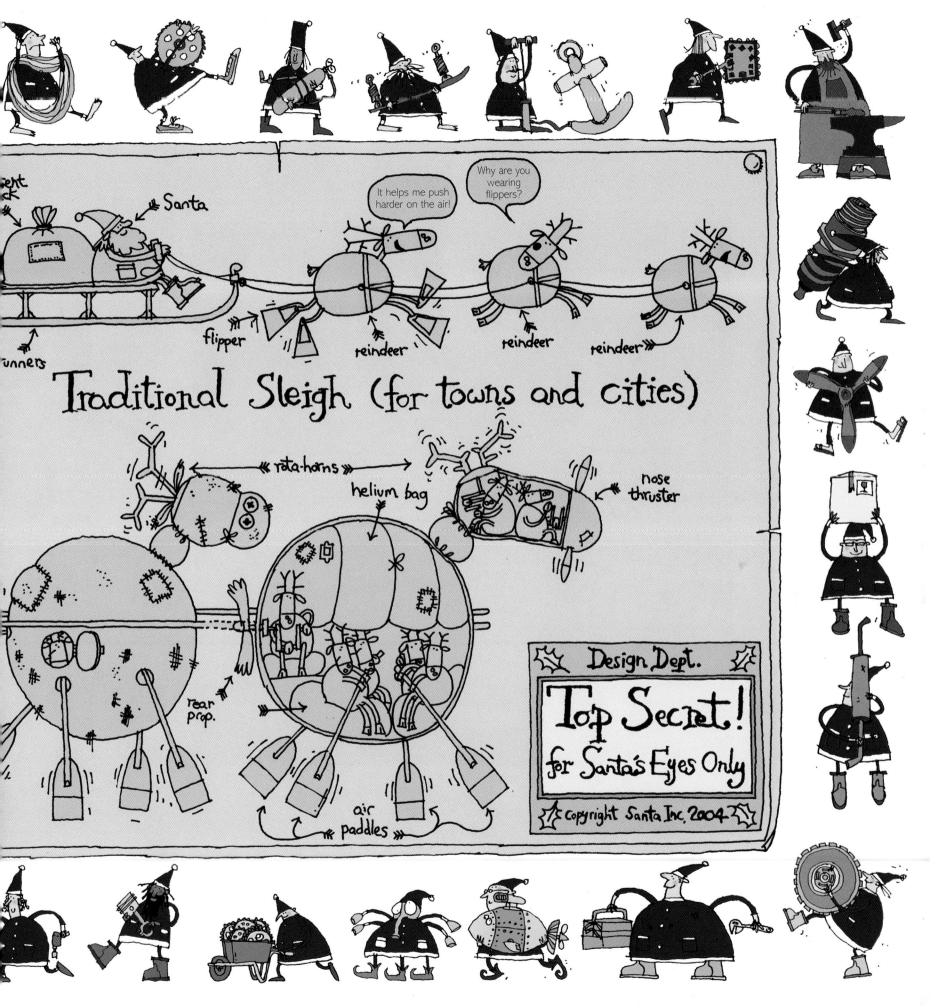

What happens then?

On Christmas Eve, at exactly 4:37 p.m., Santa sets off around the world. He starts in the east and works his way west, through all the time zones, picking up presents from the transporters when he runs low.

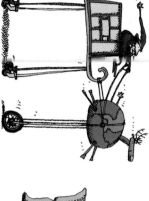
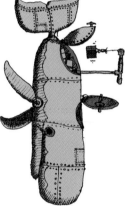
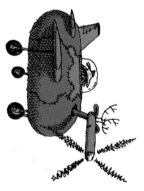

1. Set off from the North Pole

2. Deliver presents

3. Reload with presents

4. Deliver more presents

5. Repeat reloading and delivery

How does Santa get down a chimney?

Everybody thinks that Santa is very large, but in fact he is quite slim. Flying at high altitude in the middle of winter is very cold. He therefore wears a special heated suit. When he arrives at someone's home, he slips out of the suit and into the house via the chimney, door, or window.

Santa has to be very flexible to get into some people's homes, so during the year he does lots of bending and stretching exercises (he is very keen on rock climbing and yoga). This keeps him fit and supple. He is in good shape for a man of his age.

What time does Santa come?

It is difficult to be precise, but you can be sure that it will be when you are asleep.

Santa is very, very fast. Each house is allocated an elf who checks to see if everybody is asleep. When the coast is clear, the elf will signal to Santa that it is safe to deliver the presents. Santa makes his delivery, and the elf moves on to another house.

What happens if you wake up?

Because Santa likes to keep it secret that he is slim, he has an emergency suit that he triggers if you do wake up. It inflates with helium, which is lighter than air and so aids his speedy escape up chimneys.

If you leave out a treat for Santa and his reindeer, it will help him complete his deliveries. Don't leave out too much, however, because if everybody does, it will not be long before Santa gets stuck in a chimney somewhere.

Christmas Day!

In the early hours of Christmas Day, Santa sets off on his return journey home. Then children start to wake up. Santa will sometimes put some small presents in children's bedrooms for them to open as soon as they wake. Or he will put them in a stocking if one is put out for him. He likes to leave the bigger presents under a Christmas tree if he can find one. This is so everyone in a family can share in the opening together.

Waiting for everybody to get up and get ready to open the big presents is probably the hardest thing for children to do all year. It is often more than children can bear. Moms and dads take forever getting coffee first. And then the old aunties insist on handing out the presents very, very slowly. This should never under any circumstance be allowed.

The best part of Christmas, after opening the big presents, is playing with them. Good children tend to get what they ask for as long as it's not too expensive or dangerous. This cannot be said of bad children. In days of old, Santa would leave lumps of coal for bad children. These days he tends not to be so harsh, but it is worth being good . . .

Because you never know what might happen if you are not...

What do Santa and the elves do on Christmas Day?

They have a Party!

And then they go to bed . . .

for a while. . . .